The Grouse and the Mouse

Emily Dodd & Kirsteen Harris-Jones

This is the story of Bagpipe the Black Grouse and Squeaker the Wood Mouse.
Bagpipe was admiring his reflection.

"Look at my lovely red eyebrows," he said. He wiggled his eyebrows at Squeaker. "It must be awful to be so dull and brown. Take one of my beautiful feathers to brighten yourself up!"

"Thanks," said Squeaker.
"But I like being brown.

It helps me to hide in the earth...

… and hide in the trees.

Brown is brilliant for a wood mouse like me."

"Have you seen my magnificent tail?" said Bagpipe.
He wiggled his bottom at Squeaker. "It must be
awful to have such a bendy tail. You need a stick to
straighten it out!"

"Thanks," said Squeaker. "But I like my bendy tail.

It helps me to climb…

…and swing…

…and balance.

Bendy is best for a
wood mouse like me."

"Just watch me fly!" said Bagpipe. "It must be awful to be so slow
and stuck on the ground."

"I like the ground," said Squeaker. But Bagpipe wasn't listening.
He was too busy taking off…

WHOOSH!

"LOOK OUT!" cried Squeaker.

CRASH!

Bagpipe smashed into the fence.

He pulled.
And he pushed.
And he wriggled.

But Bagpipe was
stuck.

It started to rain.

"Help," said Bagpipe in a very quiet voice.

"Help!" he said in a slightly louder voice.

"HELLLP!" he wailed.

"Shall I try to pull you out?" asked Squeaker.
Bagpipe nodded.

So Squeaker pulled. And he pushed. And he wriggled. But Bagpipe was still stuck.

"We need something slippery!"
said Squeaker. And he scampered off.

"MOOOOO!"

Squeaker returned riding on MacMoo, the Highland cow. MacMoo walked around in circles below Bagpipe. His hooves turned the earth into sticky, brown mud.

SQUELCH! SQUELCH!

"Thank you, MacMoo," said Squeaker. He picked up little handfuls of mud and rubbed them on Bagpipe's feathers until—

SLURRRP!

Bagpipe slipped out and landed …

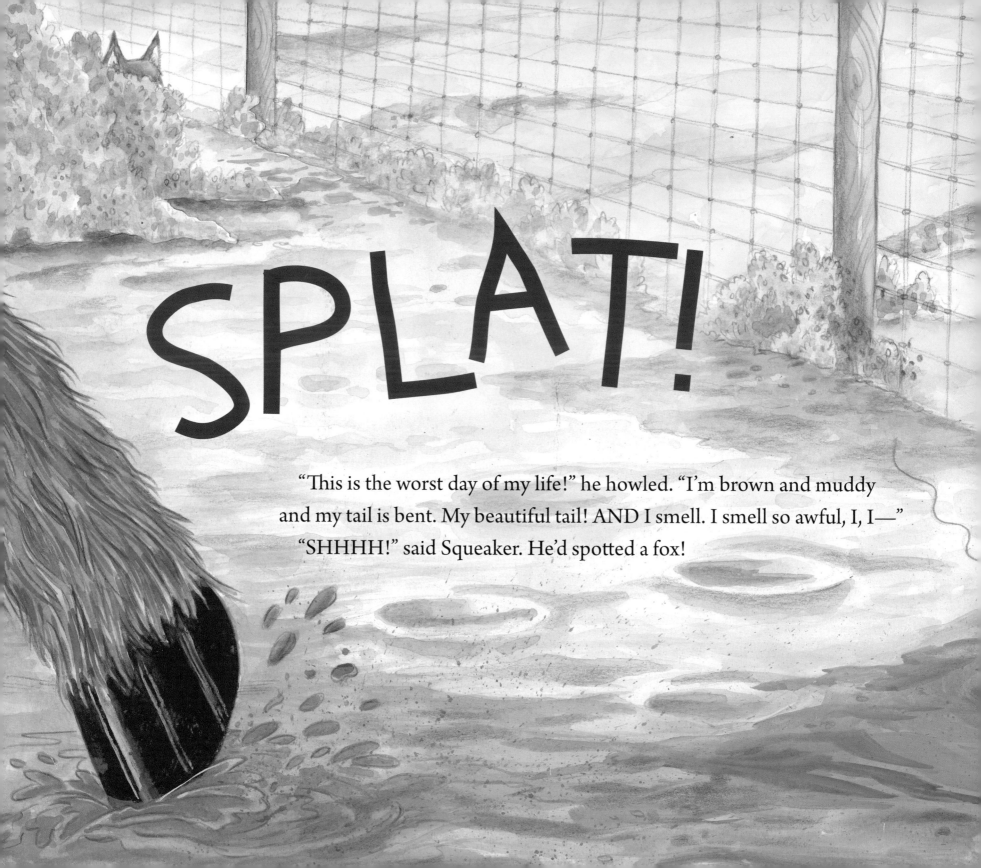

SPLAT!

"This is the worst day of my life!" he howled. "I'm brown and muddy and my tail is bent. My beautiful tail! AND I smell. I smell so awful, I, I—"

"SHHHH!" said Squeaker. He'd spotted a fox!

"GULP!" said Bagpipe, "Now I'm going to be fox food!"

The fox came closer, and closer.

"Stay very still," whispered Squeaker, "and bend over."

Bagpipe closed his eyes and lowered his head.

TROT
TROT
SWISH
SWISH!

The fox ran straight past Bagpipe with his tail waving in the wind.

Bagpipe was astounded. "The fox didn't eat me!" he cried.

"That's because he didn't see you. You're brown like the mud," said Squeaker.

"And he didn't smell a tasty grouse because you smell like MacMoo poo!"

Bagpipe laughed. "Brown really is brilliant!" he said. "And bendy was best, and I've even changed my mind about being stuck on the ground. It's a good thing I know a wood mouse like you, Squeaker!"

From that day forward, Bagpipe was a different grouse. He started to notice things: "Red squirrels have big bendy tails. Just look: they can run head first down trees! Bees, I'm astonished to say, make honey. Did you know it comes out of their bottoms!? Squeaker, what do you think will happen to this fluffy caterpillar?"

"Are you going to eat it?" asked Squeaker.

"How could I?" said Bagpipe. "When she looks like my *lovely* red eyebrows!"